Brimax Publishing

415 Jackson St, San Francisco
CA 94111 USA
Email: publishing@brimax.com.au

© Brimax Publishing, 2001
All rights reserved

ISBN 978 1 85854 726 8

Printed in China
A CIP catalogue record for this book is available
from the British library.

Schooltime for Sammy

BRIMAX

While his brother and sister got ready for the first day of school, Sammy was busy playing. He climbed his favorite tree and swung from branch to branch. Pushing books into his schoolbag, Fred called up, "You're old enough to go to school this year, Sammy."
"I don't want to go to school!
I want to stay home and play!" replied Sammy.

"But school is fun, and you'll learn all
kinds of things," said Sophie.
"I'm not going!" said Sammy, dangling upside
down and making a face. "I already know
everything. I know how to climb all the tallest
trees, and I can swing really fast.
So there! Catch me if you can!"
But Fred and Sophie didn't go after
him – they didn't want to be late for school.

Sammy spent the morning playing, but he soon got bored without any playmates.

"What's wrong, Sammy?" asked his mother, when she found him moping.

"There's nobody to play with," said Sammy grumpily.

"Well, all your friends are at school," explained his mother. "Maybe you should go, too."

"No way!" shouted Sammy, scrambling back up the tree.

At last Sophie and Fred returned home, chattering excitedly about their busy day. Sammy ran to greet them with an after-school snack.

Sammy wanted Fred and Sophie to play with him, but they had homework to do. Sammy did not want to be left out.

"I can do homework," he said, climbing onto a chair and joining them at the table.

"How many days are there in April?" Fred asked Sophie.

"Twenty-five ninety zillion!" shouted Sammy, trying to help.

"Oh, Sammy, don't be silly. We're trying to work," said Sophie with a sigh.

When Sammy's friend Jack came to visit,
he was full of news about his new school.
"The teacher is really nice, and I've learned lots
of important things," said Jack proudly.
"I know what two plus one plus two is."
"So do I!" said Sammy,
trying to count on his fingers.
"What is it, then?" asked Jack.
"It's, um, it's . . . a lot!" he answered.
"You don't know!" exclaimed Jack.

"I even learned how to write my own name,"
Jack continued. He picked up a stick.
With his tongue clenched between his teeth,
he carefully wrote J-A-C-K in the dirt.

"I can write my name, too. Look!" said Sammy.
"That's not writing, that's just scribbling," scoffed Jack.
Poor Sammy felt embarrassed.

Now Sammy was curious about school.
"What else did you do at school, Jack?" he asked.
"Well, I made lots of new friends, and we
all played games together," said Jack.

As Sammy listened, Jack told him everything
he had learned. His favorite part of the day
was Show and Tell, when people could bring in
special things and share them with the class.
"You really did do a lot,"
said Sammy with a sad sigh.

"I'll paint you a picture of a tree, if you want," offered Jack, to cheer up his friend. "That's another thing I learned today!" With his eyes open wide, so he wouldn't miss anything, Sammy watched as Jack brushed paint over a piece of paper. "That's the best picture in the whole world!" said Sammy admiringly.

After Jack left, Sammy tried to paint a tree himself, but his painting just looked like a messy blob.

That night at dinner, Sammy was very quiet.
He did not even feel like eating.
Nobody noticed, though, because Sophie and Fred
were chattering loudly about school.
"I got a gold star on my spelling test," bragged Sophie.
"I won a race at recess," said Fred proudly.
"Good job, both of you," said their mother and father.

After dinner, Sammy decided that he wanted to be as smart as his brother and sister. Very quietly, he crept over to Sophie's schoolbag and took out a book.
Sitting in a corner, he opened the book and tried to read it. But it was no use – the words just looked like squiggles to him.

When Sophie and Fred found Sammy
with the book, they read him the story.
It was a thrilling tale about pirates.

The next morning, Sammy woke up very early.
He was very excited as he searched for the
little bag his mother had made for him.
When he found it, he put Effalump,
his favorite toy, carefully inside.
He wanted to have something for Show and Tell.
Sammy marched into the kitchen
and announced, "I'm ready!"

Sammy's family looked up in surprise.
"Ready for what, Sammy?" asked his father.
"I want to go to school after all," declared
Sammy. "I want to learn how to read and write
and count and draw beautiful pictures."
"That's wonderful," said his mother.
"But first you'll need to have some breakfast."

After breakfast, Sammy set off with Sophie
and Fred, walking very quickly.
"I'm already a day late for school," said Sammy
with a grin. "I don't want to miss any more!"